Tell Tales

Peter Pan

James M. Barrie

Retold by Michael Rosen

Illustration: Francesc Rovira

Wendy, Michael and John lived in London and every night Wendy read to her two brothers or told them stories. Their favourite tales were about a boy called Peter Pan. He lived with the fairies, she said and whenever children died, Peter was with them. The children's mother remembered stories about him too and when she heard that Wendy was telling the boys about him, she said, 'He's grown up now of course.'

'Oh no, he isn't grown up,' said Wendy, 'he's just my size.'

Another time she told everyone that there were leaves off a tree in their bedroom one morning. 'I do believe it is that Peter again,' she said.

One night, when the children were all asleep, a light entered the room. When it came to rest, you could see it was a fairy, no longer than your hand, called Tinker Bell. A moment later, Peter dropped in.

'Where's my shadow?' he said.

'Over there,' said Tinker Bell.

When Peter caught up with it, he thought that he and his shadow would join together like two drops of water. When it didn't he shuddered and sat on the floor and cried.

Wendy asked Peter where he lived.

'Second on the right and then straight on till morning,' he said.

'What a funny address!' Wendy said.

'No it isn't,' said Peter.

'I mean is that what they put on the letters?' Wendy said.

'Don't get any letters,' Peter said.

'But your mother gets letters?'

'Don't have a mother,' he said.

'Oh no wonder you were crying,' Wendy said.

'I wasn't crying about mothers,' he said, 'I was crying because I can't get my shadow to stick on.'

So Wendy sewed Peter's shadow back on and Peter told them about Neverland where lost boys live.

'Will you come?' he said to them. 'I'll teach you how to jump on the wind's back and then away we go.'

Peter blew fairy dust on them and right there and then they could fly.

'Oh lovely,' Michael screamed. 'Look at me!'

'There are mermaids and pirates in Neverland,' said Peter.

'Let's go at once,' John said.

'Come,' said Peter and he soared out into the night followed by John, Michael and Wendy. Flying for what seemed like days, they came to an island.

'That's a pirate ship,' Peter said. 'The captain, Captain Hook, has a hook instead of a right hand, and he claws with it.'

'Claws?' asked John getting scared.

'A long time ago a great big crocodile bit off his hand. The crocodile wants to eat the rest of him. One day it swallowed a clock, so every time Captain Hook hears a clock ticking he is terrified.'

Now Tinker Bell was becoming jealous of Wendy getting so friendly with Peter so she flew down to see some of the lost boys.

'Quick, boys,' Tinker Bell said to them, 'Peter wants you to shoot that bird,' and a boy fired and Wendy fluttered to the ground with an arrow in her chest.

When the boys saw that it was a girl they felt terrible. A moment later, Peter arrived.

'Great news, I have brought some new friends.'

The boys stood back to show Peter what they had done. He was furious and was about to punish them and Tinker Bell when Wendy stirred. The arrow had hit a button. She was alive.

'If she lies here, she will die,' said one of the boys.

'Then let's build a little house around her,' Peter said.

So everyone, Michael and John too, hacked and chopped and carried until a safe, cosy little house was built.

Soon Wendy was well again and every
night tucked the lost boys into bed, told
them stories and sang to them.
Outside, they dressed up, playing
games in a place they called
Slightly Gulch.

Captain Hook, the captain of the ship
the children had seen the day they
arrived on the island had kidnapped a
woman called Tiger Lily. Peter planned
to set her free and one day fought hand
to hand with Captain Hook. Twice the
iron-hand clawed him, but in the end
Peter caught up Tiger Lily and flew off
with her.

Wendy and her brothers planned to go back home now. Peter ordered Tinker Bell to lead the way, but just as they were leaving, Captain Hook and his pirates made a dreadful attack. In the terrible fight that followed, the boys and Wendy were bundled up and taken off to the pirate ship. Peter escaped, went home and then fell into a dreamless sleep.

Captain Hook found Peter still asleep and added five drops of a deadly poison to Peter's cup and then ran off.

Peter woke up and raised his cup.

'No,' shrieked Tinker Bell. 'It's poisoned.'

'Don't be silly,' said Peter and started to drink. Tinker Bell got between his lips and the cup and swallowed the whole drink. In a moment, her wings could scarcely carry her.

'Now I am going to die,' she said, 'but I'd get well again if children believed in fairies.'

Peter flung out his arms.

'If you believe,' he shouted, 'clap your hands. Don't let Tink die.'

And would you know it, Tinker Bell got better.

On board the pirate ship, Wendy was tied up and the boys were going to be thrown into the sea.

'Are they to die?' asked Wendy.

'They are,' snarled Captain Hook.

Suddenly, he heard something: the terrible tick-tock of the crocodile. A great change came over him. He fell in a little heap. The sound came steadily nearer.

'Hide me,' he cried. He didn't know it was Peter, making the tick-tock noise.

But the tick-tocking faded away. Hook plucked up courage again.

'Fling the girl overboard.'

'There's none can save you now, missy,' one of the pirates said.

'There is someone,' a voice said.

'Who's that?'

'Peter Pan!' came the answer, and Peter leapt on board.

'So Pan,' said Hook, 'this is all your doing.'

'Yes, James Hook,' came the answer, 'it is all my doing.'

Without more words they started fighting. Peter was a superb swordsman. He dodged and lunged but his arm was too short to reach the captain. Hook was brilliant too and forced Peter back, but every time he thrust forward with his sword, Peter turned aside. Then he tried to get close and finish Peter off with the hook but Peter ducked under it.

Now, Hook struck out in all directions but Peter fluttered round him, as if the wind the sword made was blowing him out of danger. Finally, just as Hook turned, Peter gave him a great kick. Captain Hook went flying overboard into the mouth of the crocodile.

Now for the rest of the pirates.

'Down boys and at them,' Peter called out. If the pirates had stuck together they would have stood a chance but they ran hither and thither. Some of them leapt into the sea, others hid in dark places, until they were found and they jumped into the sea too.

Back in London, the children's mother and father missed them terribly. Peter didn't want the children to go back so he flew to London and said to Tinker Bell, 'Quick, Tink, close the window. That's right. Now you and I must get away and when Wendy comes she will think her mother has barred her out; and she will have to come back with me.'

But just then he looked in and saw the children's mother crying. So Peter opened the window again, and the children flew in.

'Will you stay with us?' said the children to Peter.

'And go to school? Grow up into a man? No one's going to catch me and make me a man.' At that he flew off into the night.